Grimm's Fairy Tales

For Auntie Mary
S.P.

For Lukas
C.J.

ORCHARD BOOKS
338 Euston Road, London NW1 3BH
Orchard Books Australia
Level 17/207 Kent Street, Sydney, NSW 2000

This text was first published in the form of a gift collection called
The Sleeping Princess by Orchard Books in 2002

This edition first published in hardback in 2012
First paperback publication in 2013

ISBN 978 1 40830 839 4 (hardback)
ISBN 978 1 40830 840 0 (paperback)

Text © Saviour Pirotta 2002
Illustrations © Cecilia Johansson 2012

A CIP catalogue record for this book is available
from the British Library.

1 3 5 7 9 10 8 6 4 2 (hardback)
1 3 5 7 9 10 8 6 4 2 (paperback)

Printed in China

Orchard Books is a division of Hachette Children's Books,
an Hachette UK company.
www.hachette.co.uk

Grimm's Fairy Tales

The Frog Prince

Written by Saviour Pirotta

Illustrated by Cecilia Johansson

ORCHARD

Long ago, there was a king who had a very
beautiful daughter. She was so beautiful,
she even dazzled the sun.

Sometimes, when the weather was warm, the princess went out in the forest and sat by a cool, deep pond.

One day she was playing with her favourite golden ball when it slipped out of her hands and sank into the water.

The beautiful princess started to wail and cry.

"Whatever is the matter?" croaked
a voice behind her.

The princess turned to see a huge frog
with bulging eyes.

"I have dropped my favourite golden ball in the well," she sniffed. "I'd give anything to get it back."

"Anything?" echoed the frog, hopping into the water.

"Promise me that you'll let me come and live with you in your palace," said the frog. "Promise I can eat from your silver plate and sleep on your silken pillow – and I'll fetch your ball for you."

So the princess smiled and promised the
frog she would take him to the palace with
her. But she had no intention of keeping
her promise.

The frog dived down to
the bottom of the pond
and surfaced with
the golden ball.

The princess took
the ball and started
to run away.
   "Wait for me,"
cried the frog.

But the princess didn't listen. She just kept
on running and running until she reached
her father's palace.

The next day, the princess was having
dinner with her father when she heard
a *plip, plop, plip, plop, plip* sound.

Then there was a knock at the door and a
croaky voice called, "Princess, princess, let me in."

The princess opened the door and, to her horror, she saw the frog sitting just outside.

The princess slammed the door shut in his face. And she told her father about the golden ball and how the frog had rescued it for her.

"A princess should always keep her promise," said the king. "Let the frog come in and give him some dinner."

So the princess opened the door again
and the frog followed her inside.

Trying hard not to grimace, the princess put the frog on the table – as far away from her as possible.

"Bring your plate closer so we can eat together," said the frog.

He licked at her food
with his tongue . . .

. . . and drank milk
from her goblet.

The princess was so disgusted that she
could hardly touch anything.

At last the frog said, "Thank you for that excellent meal. Now take me upstairs to your bed so that I can sleep."

When the princess heard this, she began to cry.

But her father grew angry and said,
"You should be grateful to anyone
who's helped you in your hour of need.
Take the frog up to your room and let
him sleep in peace."

The princess picked up the frog and, holding him at arm's length, took him up to her bedroom.

"Now give me a kiss," said the frog.
The princess was horrified!

"If you do not kiss me," said the frog, "I shall tell the king. He won't be pleased when I say you have gone back on your word."

The princess didn't want to get into further trouble with the king, so she agreed.

All at once, there was a blinding flash
of light, and the frog turned into a prince!

The prince told the princess how a horrible witch had put a curse on him . . .

. . . and how she, the princess, had broken the curse with her kiss.

At dawn the next day a beautiful carriage came to fetch the prince and take him back to his kingdom.

At the rear of the coach stood Henry, the prince's most loyal servant.

Poor Henry had been very upset when the witch turned his prince into a frog. He was so upset that the doctor had put three iron bands around his heart to keep it from breaking with sorrow.

The princess asked her father if she might marry the prince, and he agreed.

The princess joined the prince in the coach and the driver cracked his whip. The servants cheered as they set off along the street.

When the coach was some distance from
the palace, the prince heard a loud crack.

"Henry," he called,
"is the carriage
falling apart?"

"No, Your Majesty," replied Henry,
"it's not the carriage that's breaking,
it's one of the iron bands around my heart!"

There was another crack, and another. Henry yelled with joy, for at last all three bands had fallen from his heart.

Now Henry was free to celebrate the return of his prince with the princess. The wedding festivities soon began and Henry was overjoyed to see his master marry the beautiful princess.